Her Name Upon The Strand

STORIES AND PHOTOGRAPHS

Her Name Upon The Strand

STORIES AND PHOTOGRAPHS

Tammy Ho Lai-Ming

DELERE PRESS

First published in 2018
by Delere Press LLP
Block 370G Alexandra Road #09-09
Singapore 159960

DELERE PRESS LLP T11LL1061K
www.delerepress.com

Designed by Sarah and Schooling

ISBN 978-981-11-7849-8

Some of the stories in this collection first appeared, sometimes in a very different form, in the following publications. I thank their editors for giving my work an opportunity to be read.

55 Words, Arabesques Review: Contemporary Women's Literature, Berfrois, Bodega Fiction, Cha: An Asian Literary Journal, The Danforth Review, The Delinquent, Martian Lit, MiPoesias, Mud Luscious, Orbis Quarterly International Literary Journal, Quarterly Literary Review Singapore, Queen Mob's Tea House, Raft, The Standard, Stand Magazine, Strand Magazine and *Yuan Yang*.

My deepest gratitude to Jeremy Fernando and Yanyun Chen at Delere Press and to Sarah and Schooling for their meticulous care in designing and typesetting this book.

For those who understand.

'You put something down and you don't know immediately what it is.'
—John Berger

'Certainly reality is altered.'
—David Markson

'Do I wake or sleep?'
—John Keats

Meetings with Remarkable Men And Women (Selected)

i.

There was a coffee house not too far from the university library (but far enough to deter most students from taking a pilgrimage). I spent quite a few afternoons there, armed with a book or two. Thinking back, I was good at prolonging the life of a latte. I seldom paid attention to other people, and I enjoyed my anonymity. Still, I stole glances at others: some walked in wearing long black gowns that almost touched the floor; some wore masks like those on display in a Venetian souvenir shop; some carried such big sacks that I wondered if there were murdered bodies inside. I was minding my own business one afternoon, possibly reading a book about medicinal cannibalism, a man who smelt exactly like another man I'd met in Krakow (a distinctive mixture of cooked pork fat, expensive hair mousse and old leather) sat next to me and immediately drew his bulky armchair closer to mine. Despite myself, I became quite shy. He was not handsome, but he was dressed smartly, although I thought the shade of grey of his suit was perhaps too bright for a middle-aged man. There was a red dot—one of those dots you see mushrooming on older people—on one of his cheeks. We sat there, next to one another, for a long while. Then he stood up, patted my head two times and left as abruptly as he sat down.

ii.

She was a tall, short-haired girl and she wore jeans that were a little too short for her long legs. Her socks—their colour I cannot now recall— were exposed with her every step. There was another girl with us, too, but I remember nothing about her except that she brought our number to three. That afternoon, unchaperoned, we found ourselves first in a playground, then, in a kind of grassland. All of a sudden, someone (not me) took out a small cooking pot, and we started to make soup out of handfuls of unwashed grass. The tall girl also sprinkled some crushed purple and poppy-red petals in the pot, as well as parts of other plants I did not recognise. She did this expertly, in a theatrical fashion, as though mimicking a TV chef. I don't remember how the soup tasted, but, afterwards, when I recounted the incident to an aunt, she said that we had been silly and that we could have been poisoned and that our organs might rot. Before we departed, the tall girl, under a barren tree in a courtyard, said to me in a tone that was neither indifferent nor insincere: 'We never know how quickly a plant sprouts.' I realised much later that she was trying to sympathise with me about my height.

> ### *iii.*

To whom do you fascinatingly belong? he asked, referencing Henry James without naming him. *To the highest bidder?* he asked again, and I remained silent. A young man whose sideburns were artificially curled, he could have been a bartender or a university student or a writer plotting his third 'experimental' novel.

> ### *iv.*

My mother, a woman of virtue, is not someone you would proverbially call 'fun-loving.' I thank her dearly for that. For example, when my sisters and I were young, an uncle wanted to give us an old video game before buying a new one. My mother quickly and assertively declined the offer, believing that nothing that didn't get us to read or write or sleep could come to any good. I was only given a fake Barbie when I was hospitalised, aged six or seven, for mouth surgery—my lower lip had become infected after my paternal grandmother had accidentally kicked me from the other end of the sofa while talking on the phone. The lip grew to such a size that speaking became difficult; I now believe that that imposed bout of silence might have been the impetus for my generally quiet disposition.

The fake Barbie made me understand at least two things: 1) that dolls are truly boring and 2) that as Barbie didn't have nipples (I didn't know the word then), mine must be unnatural. On the day of my discharge, I was also given a new red dress, with a flourish of lace around the collar. But my initial elation at the gift was dampened quickly enough: it became obvious that I was only getting my Chinese New Year dress a couple of months early. On the short walk from the hospital to the bus stop, an old and seemingly kind woman was giving out balloons with smiley faces on them to sick children to cheer them up. I had been taught never to accept anything from strangers, and so when the old lady handed me a big blue balloon, I swatted it so hard with my Barbie doll, it burst. The popping sound was loud, and the woman's shocked and injured face—I was ashamed to understand, even then—suggested she thought I was rejecting her, not the balloon, not even the idea of a balloon.

Black Me

'Medium-sized, twenty-five-year-old HK-Chinese woman looking for males who are interested in listening to stories.' Succinct, revealing and yet mysterious, the advertisement yielded enough responses to keep her busy and entertained for many evenings.

Her parents were oblivious to her secret predilection. They thought she was studying some obscure Oriental languages. Thousands of them were approaching extinction; someone must record, archive and mourn them. These were what the parents thought their daughter was doing. 'She's so noble.' They said in awe to relatives during Chinese festivities. Some of the relatives were impressed. Some shook their heads: 'Why bother?'

A few candles were lit in her living room one autumn night. The man, thick-lipped and bald, was investigating the texture of the greenish blue sofa. The large clock on the wall reported discreetly that the time was fifteen to eleven. Impatience was building up in her belly. 'Do you want me to tell you a story?' She finally uttered the question. The man said: 'I don't know.'

This is weird. You invite me to your house to listen to a story?

Yes.

She first told the story of Athena, the goddess of virgins. Athens was her favourite city; the owl was her favourite bird; the olive was her favourite tree. She was inside the stomach of her mother, Metis, and also the forehead of her father, Zeus. She was creative and brave.

I know this story already. Can you tell me something new?

It was good that he asked. The roles were switched now. Each had begged the other for something.

Of course everyone knows their Greek mythology. Some of the narratives are reincarnated in modern films, art forms and poetry. Some writers reinterpret the myriad well-known stories and cash in huge sum of currency. The best part of the night for her was that she could tell a story, sometimes more, of her choice and imagination.

That night, after Athena, she told the man the story "Black Me":

It's about a woman who was commissioned to blacken things. These 'things' included travel guidebooks which were from the ancient times, video clips which displayed different mannerisms of snoring, the deepest secrets of the most deeply-hurt hearts, hazel eyes, fruits that had gone bad with worms crawling on the skins, etc. One day, when the woman was working at her secluded house as usual, a man knocked on her door. She opened the door and allowed the black wind to stir the rim of her black skirt. He showed her a thin book and a blue backpack. The colour blue almost immediately dissolved into the overwhelming black background. He asked her for a favour. She stared at him half-relieved, half-scared.

What's in the backpack?

Someone has said that if you mention a gun at the beginning of a short story, you must make sure that there will be a gunshot somewhere in the story. Is that true?

She was still asleep when her mother touched her forehead and checked if it was iron-hot like two hours ago.

What is this?

The man interrupted, not at all unperplexed.

Black Me.

It's not. Where does this 'mother' come from? I want to know what's in the backpack and why the woman was 'half-scared' of the man.

After the man had left, her mother materialised in the woman's mind uninvited. She made up encounters that they might have had. For example, when she's ill her mom might have tenderly measured the temperature of her forehead with three well-polished fingers. That's a reassuring thought.

But at the back of her head she knew that they were never on good terms. She hated her mother ever since she realized that she was being given boy's clothes, all black in colour, on purpose. Her mother was a young mother who didn't want her daughter to dilute the praises which were once solely for her. She would trim her daughter's hair short and neat every other week: the sizzling teeth of the scissors crisscrossed between strong black strands. This way, her daughter would look like an orphaned boy.

What's inside the backpack? Who was the man? What did he want?

The man was speaking louder than before.

When she was two and a half her mother sent her to a nursery school. There was a gutter not far away. The kids, for some unknown reasons, were fascinated by the black water in the gutter; they would play with the water when the parents were not looking. They did not know where the water was from or if the water was suitable for drinking. But they knew that if their parents witnessed them touching the slimy liquid, then loud screams involving lots of vibration from vocal chords would be ensured. It was such a piece of commonly accepted knowledge that even the least mentally developed kids would pay attention to their parents' gazes before attempting to squat next to the meandering black river. She was not very different from other kids. When she was waiting for her mother to pick her up, she would lie down on her stomach, face down, stretch her arm and dip a finger in the shallow water and draw shapes of Easter eggs on the calm surface. Sometimes hours passed in the scum. She pretended she was content, even though she was bored, cold, and afraid.

What happened to the man?

The man insisted.

What man?

The man who gave the girl a thin book and a blue backpack! Have you forgotten him?

She pondered at the question for a moment. No she had not forgotten the man. In every story that she told there must be a man, some men, or a lot of men. They come and go, as if in real life.

The contents of the blue backpack were generously displayed on her
working desk: there was a miniature Chinese sword with carvings of wing-
spread dragons. The sword looked rustic, yet sharp. There was also a black
and brown Burberry scarf which could use some ironing. There was a
small bottle of half-empty ENVY perfume, a jar of yellowish hand-cream,
a red packet with the Chinese word 'Fortune' gold-pressed on it, a small
box of MAX staples, a crumpled postcard featuring four rabbits walking
with their hind legs like gorillas, a Thailand key-ring, a Leon Lai CD, a
disgusting-looking ball of black hair, a bar of soap, some tattoo stickers,
an orange rubber band, a flat piece of stone, a timer…

I think you have quite enough items.

The man interrupted. She was going to stop listing anyway. It was late—
the crescent midnight moon beautifully lit the sky beyond the curtains. The
man was now interested in the story like a hunter might be curious to see
how a she-wolf he shot limped on the fringe of a forest or died of thirst.
Now how was she going to proceed the story?

She was made to wear black; even in the years when white or yellow were
trendy. This unitary colour scheme was first insisted by her mom, but
later she was too used to black to complain or to change her style. Shirt
to socks, pens to rings, everything's black. No other colours could be
accommodated in her life. It was only natural that she was interested in the
cryptic advertisement in the local newspaper: 'Small company seeking new
blood to blacken things. Contact Ms Black at 9400 9146 for details. High
pay.' Was it a message for selective freaks?

Are you Ms Black?

Of course not.

But I recognise your phone number.

Not everything in a story has to be fictional.

That's interesting.

Every Wednesday a large black bag was sent to her. She would start
blackening the things inside. By Friday she would return the bag with
the same items—thoroughly blackened—to the main quarter at Central.
Sometimes, when the objects required to be blackened were invisible,
non-physical, or too big (like a human being), or too abstract (like a lost
coloured dream), she would need to travel to the company and process
the objects there. But after working for the company for eight years, she
had bargaining power: now she only worked at home, and everything was
sent to her, including the most unbelievable items such as an eye, a heart,
and a sneer. If you think you understand the physics of everything, think
again. She loved her job because of the infinite supply of bright black
ink lined in presumptuousness at her front door every other Wednesday,
together with a big bag of work. The colour of the ink was significantly
darker than the seawater.

The man wanted to have something of his blackened.

She remembered what had happened many afternoons ten years ago.
No unknowns stood for his hairy chest. She knew his every detail and
quest. Constant love perpetuated his conscious desire for more of the said
flippant object. He was prepared to do anything for her.

Her mother's breath was no longer hot because she no longer breathed.

Sirens were heard and one particular purple body with blotches of red
was removed from a window-side couch to an almost concealed black
vehicle. The man packed everything in a whirlwind state of nerves—he
carried with him a reputation of a suspect and a bag of belongings of the
deceased woman. He must go to a remote land, and never to come back.
Even in shower he had to pose like a villain in order to get himself into
the character.

But today he came back with the suppressed knowledge of the puzzling
murder. 'You know I know you know I know you know'. He said to
her, speaking like a hallucinated patient and blatantly plagiarising a line
from Thom Gunn's poetry. He was once the protector but he was now a
blackmailer. 'Blacken something for me. Or else I tell.' 'You should contact
the company. They have a licence.' 'I can't afford the price. I saw the ink.
You must have some secret inventory.' 'What do you want blackened?'
'You.' 'But this is violent.' 'Yes it is.' 'Can't you do this less brutally?'

'Can't you just say Yes?' 'Why this urge?' 'I can't live.' 'Why can't you?' 'My wife.' 'Your wife.' 'I love her.' 'You love her.' 'Sometimes she enquires about my past. I can't lie.' 'You can't lie.' 'You cannot exist.' 'I cannot exist'. 'You are my recurring nemesis.' 'Nemesis.' 'Don't you blacken people's nemeses?' 'I do.' 'Do me this favour.' 'I'll do this.' The sound of the word echoed in her ears: do do do, you you you, do do do, true true true, do do, do you, true, who, do who, do you who do you true few too, do you too, do you through, do you two do you two true screw you to blue do you

That night, she wrapped herself in a black blanket and poured icy black ink onto herself. At the same time there was a black hole in the man's memory. The hole would be irrefillable. Always, like a vagina.

That's it?

Yes.

The man sat silently on the greenish sofa. Thinking, formulating questions, doubting. She loved telling nonsense stories. It was fun and satisfying.

Tomorrow she would tell a story about a medieval girl who was in so many carnivals that her parents no longer recognised her. That would be largely autobiographical.

I Hope One Day You Will Learn How To Use The Oyster Knife

I make a list of things I don't know: 1) The precise hue of your beard when you're pouring me wine. 2) The name of the kind of bread you bake. 3) The probably obscene words you scribbled next to a Shakespearean sonnet when you were young. 4) Where did you buy those checkered pants? 5) How to eat such a huge and juicy apple you give me. 6) The difference between a heavy raindrop and a snowflake seen on a languishingly moving bus. 7) The wettest months in your home town, known for the shells and Yeats. 8) When you're snoring in metrical beats, what enters your mind? 9) Were the first pair of chopsticks you used made of ivory, wood, or steel? 10) The accurate lexeme to describe the softness of your lips. 11) The physics explaining why it's pleasing to see a paperback sitting in your hand. 12) If you cooked cloud ear mushroom for other friends. 13) The duration of time you spent on selecting the perfect hair dryer for me. 14) The variety of cocktails you've invented as a bartender. 15) When we were in your favourite café (cute Victorian prints on one wall), were you disappointed that I didn't know how to order a latte? 16) Whether you like the overwhelming verbal attention I'm giving you. 17) How was it possible that we missed Apollinaire's grave, you fool? 18) The location of that mysterious full body mirror you claimed you own. 19) The length of your DNA remaining in a girl's mouth after you've kissed her for the first time, hungrily, in your living room.

Dreams

i.

I had a weird dream the other night, possibly inspired by the Brexit vote. In the dream there was a referendum about whether books should be universally banned. In the end, more people voted for the motion than against it, and so the world became officially bookless. In this new order, I belonged to a secret group, very much like in *Fahrenheit 451*, who memorised texts, and turned ourselves into walking and breathing books. But not all members could choose which books to read and become. And so I was assigned to be porn. And regardless of which members in the secret group came to me to release my book memory, I had to oblige.

ii.

I had a dream that some might consider sexy. In it, I applied to be a high-end escort and on the application form I ticked 'SM possible'. So I was given some training. The male instructor made us watch some SM-inflected porn, and then ordered us to take off our clothes. I noticed that the other women were wet, aroused by what they'd seen. I, instead, found myself bleeding (in reality I was having a heavy period) so I said I am sorry but I cannot go on because it is my time of the month. Upon hearing this, the trainer, beaming, said, 'That is great. You and I can do something very special indeed. I will teach you.' I got very scared and uncomfortable, and said that I was suffering great period pain (I was in real life as well). And so I fled, ran as fast as I could out of the training barn and onto the grassland. With each step, my blood stained the white and yellow flowers.

Let Her Go

On Christmas Eve, 24th December 2004, she did not get the pink Vivienne Westwood handbag he had promised, but she said it was all right. In the hotel room, after ejaculation, he was combing her long black hair with his fingers and she was scratching her left forearm. It was winter and yet, strangely, mosquitoes bit. They remembered that more Christmas songs were sung before the handover. Now people sang the National hymn.

He switched the television off. They only needed it for about half an hour, to cover the noises they made which were at first gentle and then deep, intense. He said he loved the smell of the hair under her arms. He said her eyes were of the shape of almonds. He said it felt comfortable to hold her small body. He said many things.

The bedclothes had Japanese characters on them. She tried to read the characters but it was difficult. Then she began to make up sounds to cope with the eccentric shapes. It was better than counting sheep to sleep.

The door was open. He could see her naked body clearly. She did not know she should be shy. He did not do it on purpose. Her hair was at last tamed by the water from the nozzle. Who didn't make mistakes?

That year he was eighteen and she was six.

The next morning they both woke up early. She drew the curtains apart and when she looked down she could see some crazy people swimming in the oval swimming pool, wearing bikinis. The industrial buildings in the background were giving out black smoke as early as half past six in the morning. Tsuen Wan was one of the abandoned city roses planted by the government and the Panda Hotel was one of the cheapest yet decent hotels he could afford. He was in his black boxer shorts now. His legs were bony. His big toes were round like marbles that children played with. From the windows she walked back to him; she climbed on the bed and rested her head on his shins. Her hair covered half of her face; the strands stirred a little with her breathing. They lay on the bed just like that for about fifteen minutes until he had a strong urge to pee.

When she woke up again she saw a room without him. She got out of bed and looked at herself in the mirror instinctively. She was happy, if tears and messy hair were happy. A week later it would be the end of the year. The year of the Rooster was coming. He would become thirty-nine and she twenty-seven.

He bought her a black dress once. There was a silver Earth on the front. America, Canada, Africa, Germany… She was wearing that dress when he brought her to the cinema. They watched a movie about giant monkeys. Was it Congo? After the movie, it was rather late, and they ate in a small Western restaurant. He taught her which spoon to use for soup and which spoon to use for ice cream. He showed her how to use a knife and fork to cut steak. He ordered lemon tea for her. When she smiled, he knew he was not treating her as his niece. She was innocent. No one should know about this growing, peevish love.

She stayed in the hotel room until it was time to check out. It was Christmas Day, a Saturday. But despite the 'red' on the calendar he had to work. Suppose he was not needed at work, what would they do? She would like to watch *Possession*, or any other thing that had to do with the notions of love or history. She buttoned her brown shirt. He had forgotten his watch. It was on a small table next to the bed, together with two empty glasses and an unlit, fake, broken, Victorian lamp. A sense of helplessness ate her up. It had been so long but he was using the same watch as yesterday, yesteryear… She picked up the watch and put it in her palm. The watch said it was a quarter to twelve.

He had moved away with her grandparents and aunts. She saw him less and less. Sometimes she looked at the pictures that they drew together. One was a picture of an ocean. The ocean was sea blue. There were lots of fish in it. There were also some starfish and seashells and long seaweed at the bottom. The fish had different patterns and colours: spotted, checked, horizontal stripes, vertical stripes, plain … Then the boys at school made her forget all about him, but the pictures were kept tidily in a wooden trunk under the bed.

It was 1999. On Christmas she went to a Christmas party with some friends she met in university. For the occasion she wore a low-cut white woollen top, a purple leather miniskirt and a pair of long tight boots that reached the knees. It was well after midnight

Her phone rang. It was not him but Marco. How could it be him? Every time after some secret and passionate sexual exploration, he had to keep himself away from her for at least two days. In those two days or more, she was always worried that he was with someone else, or worse, that he would rather be on his own. Last week when they were together, he told her a dreadful story he read in the paper about a single mother who had cancer and died. Her children had to live on the streets. 'Why is life full of misery and suffering?' he asked. 'Poverty, hunger, all kinds of sicknesses…' She clutched his arm, and they gently kissed. The bleak outside world was distant, not immediate. Now she could not help but think that falling in love, especially love that did not have a future, was miserable. 'This relationship isn't going anywhere,' she thought. To speak and think of relationships in terms of journeys was to reduce the two grown humans involved to two ants.

He said he had been thinking of her all of the time. He said he knew she liked him, and she did not need to be convinced otherwise. He said now she was old enough to make decisions. He said no one should know about this growing, peevish love. He said many things. That night she took out the pictures from the old trunk.

A few weeks later. This was how the first time they gave pleasure and pain to the other. She was on her back, naked and shy, her legs would not part no matter what. When he mounted her, their bodies blurred. He did not break her on that night, but the contact of his chest and her breast was enough to make him crazy. Her tender middle was caressed by where he sprang. Was it shame? She cried and cried afterwards, even though no real harm was actually done. But by all means, he saw her body with a triangle of dense fur that was not there when he last saw her.

Marco was her boyfriend, known to her friends and family. Marco wanted to have Christmas dinner with her. She said yes. Love was with her but so was guilt.

He fell in love with her when her youth was excessively dominant and her sexual attractiveness was blissfully praised by the gaze of walkers-by.

For a fleeting moment she thought of calling Marco back and cancelling the date. But she did not want him to think her flighty. She left the hotel and got on a bus to Causeway Bay. She bought some new clothes in Apple Mall which she frequently visited and after that she rushed back home to have a shower and wash her hair. Going out with Marco was different. The hair had to be right and cosmetics should be appropriately put on the face. She enjoyed this lack of casualness that kindled the coyness and nervousness in her.

He put a hand on her face. Without lipstick, her lips were so pale, almost white. She breathed softly. He thought her nose was too big for the rest of her features. Now he could not believe he possessed her. How stupid of him to think that she would stay young forever and her heart would never turn to others. He wept, and touched her fair breasts again. From his sister, he knew her plan to go to San Francisco with Marco, her boyfriend. Perhaps he wanted to place his hand over her nose and mouth until he could not feel any moist warmth. And then he would stab himself with a knife—right into the heart—and let the blood run on and dissolve into the red Turkish carpet. He did not want to lose her to someone else. But it was selfish of him not to let her go. She liked stealing the sheets and winding herself into them tightly. It was about four in the morning; he rolled over and began to make love to her. She purred when she came. Two hours later, they woke up. When he stretched his arm to pull some sheets to his side, she got out of the bed and walked to the windows.

When she first told Marco about him, Marco was very angry. But Marco was more sympathetic when he knew her more. Marco asked her to leave her uncle and follow him to a new place to start a new life. She said yes to this request. It was not too difficult to utter that one syllable, was it? Why, Marco, why do you forgive me? she asked. 'I like *Amelie*, and watching inferior movies is shameful and intolerable' was Marco's reply. She did not understand.

Pillow Books

[1] *Things that quicken the heart/give you goose bumps*—A Saturday morning latte, sprinkled with nutmeg. A cup of warm red wine infused with cinnamon. The wails of the neighbour's cat—more human than feline. The alarm at 2.00 a.m.

The thud of an Amazon book landing at the stoop. The lights coming down at the theatre. The opening chords of "Helplessness Blues."

[2] *Things that rise*—Banana bread. The sun, every morning, even though I may not see much of it. Boiling water. Friends' pregnant tummies. A dozing cat roused by a distinctive sound. Nipples aroused by a distinctive touch.

[3] *A thing that surprised me at first*—Being called 'luv' by a complete stranger.

[4] *Mysterious things*—How one supermarket can close at five, when its neighbour closes at nine. The difference between brands of washing powder.

What a partner sees when he goes running alone.

A photograph of my family which cannot be deleted from a memory card and follows me from camera to camera.

[5] *At seven o'clock last night*, my partner returned from work. He stood outside the door, adjusted his red scarf and then walked away to get the milk he always forgets. Ten minutes later, he reappeared with a Tesco bag, claiming he had come straight from the train and had only now just arrived. I was highly suspicious, especially since he smelled faintly of beer. It did not occur to me until later that there is no Tesco nearby.

[6] *Memories of my grandfather*—Peanut-buttered bread. Empty peanut-butter jars, scraped nearly clean, lined up on the far end of the table. His wooden staff. Him, sitting alone on a bench in the playground. His smile when he saw my sisters and I skipping rope.

[7] *Infuriating things*—A person you are fond of turns out to be far less worthy than you thought. Discovering that an image you thought original has been used before.

Delayed trains. Departing trains that squeak too loud.

Someone's underwear—visible beneath his loose jeans. A still-lit cigarette thrown in a bush.

When you are wearing your tallest heels and the elevators in the Russell Square station aren't working so you have to climb the 117 steps.

When receiving guests in your house, you see a cobweb that you had not noticed before.

Fine hair above the lip. Shadows that bear little resemblance to their owners.

A recalled library book. A paper clip that doesn't clip. A zigzag in a pair of stockings that leads everybody to speculate on its cause.

An inadequate supply of chilli oil at dim sum. After you spill wine on your keyboard, and the keys stick and produce random letters.

[8] *The electronics graveyard in the closet*—Three digital cameras. Every generation of iPod. Headphones. Discordant cords. Keyless keyboards. Wireless mice. Once loved brands, now out of favour.

[9] *One day a Jehovah's Witness came to the door* and promised to return with a Chinese bible. The next day he delivered the book as promised, and he asked when he should come again. When I told him 'in one year,' the disappointment on his face almost made me convert.

[10] *Things that someone else takes care of*—Hair mice in the shower drain. Contact lens cases. Leftover soup in a Nissan cup noodle. The cup itself. Orange peels. Fallen leaves that sneak past the door. A dead spider.

[11] *Kinds of days*—Dewy days. Due days. Productive days. Reproductive days. Redo days.

[12] *Things that sadden the heart*—That each lover is not a recapitulation of all those loved before and after. A white cloth that is no longer white. A hole visible when the nail is pulled out. The removed second place setting at a table for one.

[13] *Things that give me pleasure*—It is pleasing to unexpectedly discover a particular Cantonese dish you love on the menu of a local restaurant.

Seeing herons along a bridge. Deleting junk emails *en masse*. Returning a dropped coin to its owner. Brushing my teeth for five minutes, undisturbed. Seeing my mom comb her thick hair like a young girl. Feeling the stubble on the sweetheart's face.

When the pot of morning coffee turns out perfect, not too bitter or too watery.

That every day is not like the next. That as John Steinbeck said, 'Nothing good gets away.'

When my name is uttered softly or raindrops on the windowpane doodle a letter.

Well-worn boots.

The smell of new books. The smell of old books.

Being praised, even stutteringly. Being admonished by someone I love and who means well. Being reminded of something in a timely manner.

Listening to my father sing old Mandarin songs, perfectly-pitched and confident—something which has not happened for three years.

[14] *Things to have when sleeping*—The light on. Two bottles of water. A stifling number of blankets. Six pillows to my partner's one, including two orthopaedic. Soft-covered books which can double as pillows in an emergency.

Summer

When I went home there she was. In the kitchen preparing an afternoon feast for my sisters and me. Sometimes fried rice with eggs. Sometimes Chinese soup with cabbage and mushrooms. Sometimes (but very rarely) sausages and slices of canned pineapples. My grandma was extremely sweaty and honestly she did not smell good. Summers were awful. Her armpits were always wet. Some white hair stuck on her forehead. The air conditioner did not help. She could not breathe smoothly with the air conditioner on.

That was the time when she was healthier. Later my grandma was so sick that she had to stay in a home for the elderly. She could no longer cook for us. The kitchen does not have her silhouette. The air conditioner is always turned on in the house in summer. But it is too cold now.

Every Saturday I went to see her. I sat next to her on her tiny but comfortable bed. There was not much to say. Conversations never really set foot. But I often imagined that elsewhere the two of us were chatting. The fact was she looked at me with a smile, and that was almost all she could do. She was such a talkative person, but then she did not speak at all. I embraced her before I left, too aware of her smell. She did not smell good. What the hell, it was summertime.

One Sunday morning slightly before seven o'clock the phone in our house rang. My parents, my sisters and I were all woken up by the ring. Finally it was my mother who picked up the phone. Then she put down the phone. She said the doctor asked us to go to the hospital and see grandma one last time, talk to her one last time. My sisters and I quietly changed our clothes. I saw their hands tremble. Nobody wanted to say anything.

When we arrived at the hospital half an hour later there she was. Lying on the hospital bed, already dead. The room was filled with her smell. My father immediately ran out of the room. We heard him scold the doctor. That fucking bastard should have called us earlier. But my father was crying. My two sisters held their hands tightly for support from one another. My mother sat on a chair in the corner of the room and wept. I stood right next to grandma's corpse, oh old face, old hair, old fingernails.

Oh old neck, old lips, old wrinkles. I stroked her face. Old nose. Oh no. Death is so dreadful.

In the afternoon we went to the home for the elderly where my grandma had stayed. We went there to collect her belongings. A photo of grandma and my two sisters. My sisters immediately cried. A photo of grandma and my two cousins and their dog. My two cousins started to cry as well. Finally there was a photo of me. I wear makeup in the photo, smiling with all my teeth showing. On the back of the photo I had written: 'To my dearest grandma, May health be with you always. Yours, mingming'. I cried.

I always pretended she was still here. But now it is summer and her smell is lacking. Summer makes me think of my grandma. This is the first summer she is not here. Where is she now? In heaven I suppose, if there was really such a place. But I prefer she no longer exists. 'Torture, torture,' my grandma used to say, with no particular cause. I can imagine she says the same thing no matter where she is, with a sense of humour, even in a bizzare place with angels and plenty of white. I have been brainwashed. To me, heaven must have angels. Heaven is white. Thus I know heaven does not suit me. I like black.

Summer has come, not romantically but anxiously. In Hong Kong it seems that every summer is hotter than the previous one. I am wearing a tube top. Nobody knows why Hong Kong has become such an uncomfortable place to live in. Even laughter needs great effort.

Ankle-deep Red Firecracker Papers

On the train from Guangzhou to Hong Kong, my handwriting looks strange. I have not written like this, in a notebook, for a long time.

By 'this', I mean writing and striking words out—aggressively I must add—and inserting new ones here and there. The result is a messy page. Even as I am scribbling this very sentence, I am aware that it may be crossed out.

This morning, I took the first train from Hong Kong to Guangzhou. Arriving at Hung Hom station near where I live at half past six to make sure that I would be able to buy a ticket for the 7:25 departure, I found a queue of people waiting to check in. They looked unhurried, unconcerned.

It was as if they had made the same trip hundreds of times.

Late November. Some people were wearing heavy jackets in anticipation of the colder weather across the border but some were still dressed in light clothes, holding on to the very last sentiments of Autumn.

A student of mine at the university where I teach once wrote a story about a conductor on the train to the afterworld. The passengers do not seem to know what is in store for them: they read books half-heartedly, doze off, chat to one another, have snacks. Life as usual. The atmosphere in the train is familiar and yet foreboding. For the conductor who is used to his job, seeing children is still upsetting.

Seated comfortably and waiting for the train to depart the platform, I was reminded of the story of the conductor and the death train. We imagine death and the crossing between life and afterlife in numerous ways, if not obsessively, at least dedicatedly.

The Chinese believe, among other things, that on the way to the netherworld, one must eat a soup that will make you forget all the events of your life. The soup, every drop of it, is made from the tears one has shed in their past life: tears of joy, sorrow, excitement, and gratitude.

Wouldn't this make one remember even more?

Thinking of these stories, I sent a WhatsApp message to my sisters, telling them that I was on my way to Guangzhou.

* * *

I had meant to keep it a secret and not let any of my family know. Over the past few years, I have learnt to be very selective regarding what I tell them. If it's something trivial, such as feeling a fever coming on or being slighted by an annoying colleague, I don't bother. If it's something very important, I delay telling them as long as possible.

They have enough on their minds: both my younger sisters—twins—are married and new mothers, while my parents, now grandparents, busy themselves babysitting the young ones. At night, they go to bed early, and the following morning, the cycle repeats.

Going to Guangzhou for the day to attend a writers and translators conference would fall into the category of 'Trivial'. To put this in context: I have on other occasions omitted to tell my family about extended trips to Europe. Often they did not notice I was gone. I remained an active participant in my family's WhatsApp group, giving the impression that I was always in the city, never away.

What would life be like if digital cameras had been widely used when I was a child? So many of my memories of childhood come from photographs untidily preserved in albums, now stored in a largely disused bookcase in my parents' bedroom, just next to their bed. I embellish these photographs with invented details. I create little stories out of them.

I once invented my presence into an image of my two sisters playing in our first home. Even though I was nowhere to be seen in the photograph, I told myself that I was just hiding behind a cupboard.

Later, flipping through the pages of the album with my mother, she casually remarked that when that photograph was taken, I was not in Hong Kong—I had been sent away to live with my paternal grandmother in mainland China, as it had become too difficult for my young mother to take care of all three little girls by herself.

There is another photograph of my sisters and me standing on the concrete front yard of the compound in China where my father's extended family used to live. It was Lunar New Year and the ground was covered with broken red scraps of paper, the remnants of firecrackers, which could be heard day and night.

I stood taller than my sisters, who were on my sides. This is worth remarking, as the finite number of years I was taller than them is now far fewer than the number of years they have been taller than me. And the number only keeps expanding.

We are wearing brightly-coloured overcoats, each a fat dumpling, although in the photograph the color have been dulled by time, which has the power to dull everything but itself.

And the dresses were all overly long. My mother must have wanted them to last more than one winter. I was about four and my sisters two. That trip to China—the first we took as a family—was condensed into this one photograph. I remember nothing else: what food did we eat? Did I play with my cousins? Were we allowed to watch the fireworks? How many days did we stay? I wonder what happened to the negative.

I have realized, for a few years now, that it is unlikely that the family will ever again go to China together like we did when my sisters and I were little. We may each take separate short trips there for various reasons, but that's about it. It will, I suppose, take the death of someone important in our extended family to reunite us on a train to China, everyone wearing black.

Now writing this back in my own home and rereading the previous sections, I can't help but feel that the urge to text my sisters earlier this morning was childish. But they'd responded warmly, warning me of the rain in Guangzhou, and asking if I had a thick jacket on.

德興海味
泰和堂
JADE RESTAURANT （麵家）
翡翠茶餐廳

HOTEL WESTMINSTER
HOTEL DU PARC
HOTEL DU PARC

專業維修地圖
裝修
不鏞鐵閘、
大小工程

Portland Street
砵蘭街

Contemplating Existence

I imagine this concrete structure next to a row of outdoor dining tables in Tsim Sha Tsui to be a time machine, covered with fauna and largely forgotten. Someone from 2047 has arrived, and he says in his world, 'Hong Kong' is rarely mentioned: the name is obsolete, censored and is considered a taboo, as the city is assimilated into the rest of China. He also says that in his time, it is a known fact that there are multiple universes, and in one of the alternative ones, Hong Kong may be completely independent. He adds: 'But no one wants to find out. Things could be so much worse.'

These are the only two trees left in the city. Their leaves are very valuable and have the potential to heal and to provide comfort and soothing energy to their users, much like in Lao She's *Cat Country*. Because of this the trees are politicised, and their ownership is very much disputed. Should it be the one who sowed the original seeds? Or should it be the one who watered and nurtured them? Should it be the one who discovered the uses of their leaves? Should it be those who benefit from their shades? In the end, it is decided that the trees will be preserved in concrete, in a museum.

Poetic License

There are many things she cannot tell him, such as how he shouldn't unfurl the dishcloth directly outside the window and let the baguette crumbs dumplinged inside fall onto the former playground, now filled with construction gravel and sand. They live on the top floor of an old building, so ancient that no one bothers to clean the obscene graffiti from the walls, although one time, efforts were made to cover up the oversized penis ejaculating titian into the stairwell.

She cannot tell him how little time there actually is between one moment and the next. He would say she speaks too abstractedly and that there are people in the world who don't know what 'abstract' means, who would not have use for the word, even. 'Stop being an intellectual snob,' he would say, or she imagines he would say. In terms of languages, he has the upper hand as he knows five, and she defers to him on a daily basis. She resorts to neologisms that thrive on not-too-outrageous poetic license. 'I trusted you,' she once said when they were riding the Metro, carrying bags of Japanese instant noodles. 'I didn't feel that I would be in any form of danger, except perhaps emotionache.' He kissed the top of her head and uttered a praise that was audible only to her: 'What an interesting word you've used there.'

He knows there are things he cannot tell her. For example, that when she insists on using the mirror to see how she looks in his eyes and vice versa while making love, while making doggie love, to be precise, he is reminded of an ex who also had a predilection for the mirror, who was also petite but bigger-breasted, and who also said 'Yes' almost too quickly in conversation in a way that was in no way disrespectful. He cannot tell her for fear she would think herself merely a lucky understudy. How can you tell a girlfriend even her moans have predecessors when her ultimate worries are falling bread crumbs and coining new words to solicit kisses?

Eyes

This morning, we eat cow eyes in the dark. They are stewed, served on plates, and have a strong ginger flavour. Last week we had chicken eyes in steamed rice rolls. They looked like oversized sesame seeds. When she feeds us, Mama reminds us that she was blind too, once, when she was young. But after eating a regular diet of animal eyes, her blindness disappeared. She often assures us that the same will happen to us.

I see better than other kids, because I have one good eye. My right eye has a dark brown pupil and the white is white like a showered rabbit. But my left eye is a lake of confused mist. At least that is what Mama says. It can only see very bright lights and swift-moving objects. But otherwise it is useless—it cannot even wink.

The rest of them do not see at all. Put a rock in front of them and they will trip on it. As I am older and can see with one eye, I have much authority in the bathing hall and the courtyard. I give directions to other kids: where to get the water buckets, how to pick corn. When Mama quits the house for chores, sometimes for days, I am the one in charge.

Mama is not our real mother. How could she give birth to so many kids? But she makes us call her Mama so that we will be loyal to her. Also there is her nurse friend who visits us every week. We call her Auntie Flower. She turns our heads, waves her hands before us, and presses her palm on our hearts to see if they are beating well.

Three days ago, we got another litter. There was nothing special about this. During my ten years' stay, I have seen hundreds of kids come and go. Most of them cry in the first few days. It is always worst in the evening when their cries mix with the sounds of the night: leaves rustling, wind whispering, furniture stretching its muscles. The weaker ones don't last long. They are led, or even dragged, out of the gate by Auntie Flower in a week or so. Wherever they go, it is not home.

The day before I came here, I was collecting firewood outside our house. I saw this woman, dressed in colours I had never seen before in our village, knocking on the neighbours' doors. She did not have much luck with them, and so I was surprised that my Mom admitted her into our house. Excited, I ran back home, eager to see who she was. I handed the tree branches to Grandma, who would burn them in the stove to make us mung-bean congee for breakfast.

The woman smiled at me, and I smiled back. Grandma wanted me to help her in the kitchen. Although reluctant, I obeyed. I sat on the kitchen floor, arranging the firewood into piles of varying sizes, while eavesdropping on the conversation in the next room. I used to remember much of that conversation, but now I can only remember one word: blind.

The woman came to our house again the following day. This time it was to take me away. There was not even time for me to pack my few things. I would have liked to take the rose pin my Mom gave me on my previous birthday, or the comb which I shared with my Grandma; it had black and white hair in its teeth. From the expressions on my Mom's and Grandma's faces, I knew they didn't rejoice at my departure. They didn't cry, but I could see that Grandma's eyes were misty.

The woman told me to call her Mama. We walked on the rugged path for about twenty minutes before we were picked up by a small van driven by Auntie Flower. There were already a few other kids sitting at the back when I got on the car. I only had a glimpse of them and the door was shut. It was so dark inside the car with the curtains drawn that I can only see silhouettes. Nobody spoke. Finally, the car stopped and we were released to the courtyard of a big wooden house. I was shocked to see the other kids there. Some of them crawled on the floor like wild animals. Some sat still like statues, facing one another without knowing it. Some had deep scratch marks on their faces, trails showing previous explorations of their skin. I was five then, and I didn't know there were people who were blinder than I was. I had never been so happy.

One day a week we play games. They are many and various. Mama tells us we need to play them to help us improve our senses of touch and hearing. But those of us who have been here long enough know the truth—that losers share the same fate with the weaker kids: they too will be led out the gate by Auntie Flower. Mama told me long ago that I do not need to participate if I don't want to. But I often play. It is fun when you never lose.

After breakfast, we play hide and seek. Mama gives the other kids five minutes to hide in the house before she will start hunting. Today, I am allowed to stand at the door and say 'Go'. I enjoy watching the kids try to rush through the door into the house. There is a lot of pushing and yelling, and some kids even trip over others as they run towards their hiding spots. Of course, the older kids know all the good places and move confidently towards them, counting their steps along the way. Others feel desperately for space between pieces of furniture, judging whether it is big and deep enough to squeeze into. Those few that have sharp hearing and have been through many games, don't hide far from the door. Instead they will wait for Mama's footsteps and then creep away when they approach. As always I find it quite funny to watch the clueless kids. Many are trying to hide under the dining table, their arms and legs exposed, or behind the curtains hoping to blend in with the wrinkled fabric. Every now and then one kid stands next to the lamp, hardens the body, acts inanimate.

Today, something else catches my good eye. One small girl from the new litter seems to move with ease through the house. She avoids obstacles—the wooden chairs, the table, the broom, the big plastic dolls on the floor—like a champion. Her skill and the fact that she appears to be having fun bother me.

Mama walks slowly, in no hurry to find the kids. The new arrivals and some of the younger kids are giggling in their little corners, amused by the dramatic suspense. Others hold their breath, careful not to betray their location. But I have no heart to watch them. I only want to know where the new girl is hiding. I tiptoe around the house, checking all the best hiding spots. But I do not see her.

By the time I have checked everywhere, Mama has already caught three kids to end the game. Two of them are crying, clearly frightened. The third is new and has no idea what his future has in store.

For the rest of the day, I cannot contain my curiosity and I search endlessly for the new girl. When I finally spot her walking into the toilet, I follow. She turns her head and smiles at me, showing her big rodent teeth. I know then with absolute certainty that she can see too. The question is, how well? I wait for her to finish and confront her. I look down into her eyes. Her left eye blinks once, twice, but the right one is chaotic, a splash of ink.

* * *

Three weeks have passed and I am still not used to having another one-eyed girl in the house. I hate it when she smiles every time our good eyes meet, as if we share a special bond.

Today is game day, and I am excited when Mama announces that we will play the marble game after lunch. This is my all-time-favourite. We play it in the open courtyard, and I am normally in charge of moving the bamboo baskets and the large potted plants to make room. Then Mama selects ten to fifteen kids and makes them sit at the far end of the courtyard, spread out like the Chinese character 'one'. Then from the other end, she rolls marbles, some quickly, some more slowly, in the kids' direction. To win, a kid must listen carefully and catch one of the marbles as they roll pass. Of course, Mama always throws fewer marbles than the number of participants, which leaves a couple of them empty-handed at the end of the game.

I quickly finish my lunch, a fish eye omelette with fried rice, and start moving the baskets and pots in the courtyard. But Mama stops me, saying that today we are playing a different version of the game. An hour later she takes us all down to the empty and windowless basement, a place I rarely go because it is always pitch black. I almost jump when Mama speaks softly into my ear. Her voice, so familiar yet so strange, chills me. She says today I should play.

A moment later, Mama is no longer standing next to me. I hear she announces something from some distance away. Then I can hear great commotions around me, but I cannot see a thing. I feel a hand forcefully pressing my head, and I am sitting on the cold floor, facing more darkness. Some more mumbling at the other end, and there is a huge splashing sound—I know the marbles have just been poured onto the floor. And I am to grab one of them.

I straighten my ears, but the others are too fast.

* * *

It is not the silence that I dread, but the ultimate disclosure of truth. I have wondered, many times before, where do all those kids go? But I never cared to look. It was someone else's fate. Now, in this butcher's shop, I can see the truth. Somewhere, tonight, a rich woman will eat human eyes in the dark.

Moments Not Resolved

My husband accidentally strangled me when we were both sleeping. The next morning he found me breathless on our small bed. Autumn wind chilled the room, unforgiving yet refreshing. Friday, already people were planning how to spend the long Chung Yueng Festival weekend. The city was gaining a crude sense of excitement. And I was dead.

My feelings for him were long extinct, I thought. But once again I was trapped by images of him, and images of us together, naked like ah gentle gifts—I was his and he was mine. The brute of infatuation; skin tightened, yearning to be touched. Listening to his voice when he talked to the police and my boss on the phone, I discovered the structure of more and more heart beats, frequent, interrupted. But when I pressed my hand on that embittered thing, there was no motion.

His bicycle clicked, clicked, clicked all the way to his office in Central while my body was being removed from our apartment on Hollywood Road. All of a sudden it struck me that it mattered little I was wearing my favourite silk scarf we bought from Cambodia a few years ago on our honeymoon; miniature elephants marching around my neck. What mattered was it really pained to see someone I thought I loved leaving for work like nothing had happened on the morning of my brand-new departure. If he shed any tears, I would like to have them magnified and kept in a bell jar for display like corpses of rare animals.

I wandered in our apartment for a few minutes, shadow-less, before the guest in black came and picked me up. For the first time I noticed a crack on the ceiling above our wedding bed; its shape was a lightning bolt. Books on the bookcase tilted towards the windows where the sunlight summoned; some book-pages became petals of lemon-yellow sunflowers, glowing on the dusty edges. I'd swear I saw my doppelganger in the oval-shaped mirror in the cramped living room, at least for a split second. Perhaps my profile tickled the mirror until it blurted out the memory of my face.

Death, be not proud. I mouthed Donne's words when the black guest materialised before me. He had no chariot that one could ride, no raven with feathers cursed by Athena, no scythe made of stainless steel, no

company of horse-faced guardians of the Chinese Purgatory, and he
certainly wasn't a beautiful woman as men would sometimes fantasise.
With modern attire and sleek hair Death stood next to the said mirror;
on that glassy surface there was a distinctive reflection of emptiness
and otherworldliness combined. I had a strange feeling that he did not
anticipate me to speak first; it was as if my measured calmness undermined
his authority and displeased him.

He stared at me for a good minute, and only spoke when my eyes could
no longer stand the deliberate fierceness of his and shifted an inch from his
pale thin face, the epitome of malnutrition and deficiency of passion. What
language he spoke in I could not possibly recognise. It must be something
universal and powerful—nothing was lost in translation—for I found myself
involuntarily nodding when his speech came to an end. He was to manipulate
time, space, law of physics; and let me relive moments in my life that were
supposed to be dramatic, traumatic. These moments would fit in my world
like lost past-scented pieces in a wooden jigsaw puzzle and make me complete.
He said I must resolve one of the moments before he could take me to 'the
next level of existence'. The point of all this, at that point, was steamingly
unclear. But who was I to bargain when I knew not what's going to happen?

First it was a small butterfly, wings patterned like multiple peacocks' eyes,
struggling in the tiny and lonely cup of my hands. There were butterflies,
melting, on my fingernails too; I could not rescue them from disappearing
and no one else cared. The sky was ribbon blue for celebration, white
clouds dotted sea waves. Two o'clock in the afternoon, my father's
alcoholic eyes were not on me. I set the butterfly free, leaving none of its
traces in my palms. I ran from one tree to another, ran in the grass, odour
of green, distracting myself from the absence of my father's attention. I
thought of wolves and caterpillars from fairy-tales. I thought of a hole that
might lead me to an underworld. Then with feeble legs I ran back to my
father. The woman whose bare breasts my father was sniffing was not my
mother. The browness of the nipples. He played piano on her stomach and
made her roar with laughter that was choking my ears.

They saw me and they became silhouettes evaporating into two nearby
trees, both had extensive branches and gigantic roots. Now I remembered
that afternoon, and why my father smiled scantily to me in my childhood
before he and my mother died in a car crash. Did I or did I not want to
resolve the sad relationship with my father? Death asked.

My voice was about to make an answer but I was already being brought
to a second oppressive scene. Mr Leung was droning on and on about
the history of Hong Kong, and the exact location of the five stars in
the corner of a red Chinese flag, and then he burst forth in a sing-song
manner which shocked quite a handful of sleepy students sitting at the
back: 'Hong Kong citizens are matches in matchboxes/ We pact tightly we
are united/ Together let's burn everything/ And move to another planet'.
Then he asked me to repeat what he had just said. I stood up, and at that
moment the whole class behind me screamed and laughed. There was a
large patch of red on my white Summer uniform spanning the length of
my small hips. That moment stilled with complexities of embarrassment,
hatred, dazzling self-loathing.

All junior faces then turned into a big nocturnal moon hanging over a
balcony, the stage prop we had for Romeo and Juliet. Now I remembered
the odyssey of riding on a bus and walking in a wet market to buy some
ginger for my uncle after school. The red patch was there the whole time,
not buried nor extinguished in my memory. With implacable shame I cried
till I fell asleep that night. Did I or did I not want to erase that moment of
redness in the classroom? Death asked.

Sometimes I liked to imagine, the buses I was sitting in, flew over the
Victoria Harbour, and landed nowhere. I was about to tell this to Death
but the next second I was already back in my apartment on Hollywood
road, watching my husband preparing dinner for us one last time in the
kitchen: pasta with tomato sauce and meat balls. I was remembering how
five years ago, when he pushed me onto his bed, I knew the moment had
come for us to experience beyond word portrayal of limbs overlapping,
lips overlapping, muscles overlapping, mass of flesh overlapping, possibly
also love. If minds were maps, I thought he was a skilled cartographer. But
what's wrong with us five years later? I watched him and found no love.
Hush! Perhaps no man had been able to wrap me in perpetual happiness,
glad-coloured wine. Abruptly at that moment I thought I was the only
person who could end the great void.

Night breeze touched the windowsills and I shivered. I remembered digging
my hands into the box of old clothes in the spare room and taking out that
elephant scarf. Did I or did I not want my husband to know he did not
strangle me? Death asked.

The Cat Woman

Living on Sai Street was also a cat woman who was extremely fond of stray felines as if they were her grandchildren descended from a secret lover; those with monstrous eyes seemed to attract her affection most. Every night, she carried boxes of leftover food from nearby restaurants and put them on the stone steps for the glaring creatures. In their past lives these cats must have been mistresses of carpenters or cobblers, accustomed to strolling the labyrinth of dimly-lit pavements to meet coarse people for carnal purposes. The cat woman sat on a torn brown cushion and waited, sometimes humming a song from a Chinese opera about a couple who poisoned themselves then turned into spirited butterflies. Wherever the cats gathered they were beckoned by the smell of their punctual dinner. Noisily, they approached the food and licked, chewed and swallowed the mixture of fish, rice and *bok choi*. Romantic eyes might pause admiring this harmonious scene under the halo of the foreboding streetlamp, for this kind of calm co-existence of a flock of animals and a human was unusual in the city. Half an hour later, when all was consumed, the cats vanished into the obscurity of back alleys, still miaowing beyond human decipherability.

Observations

My love for you is not like new linens—nice for the first week but shrinking after the first wash.

'If' is the French for yew. A coniferous tree.

I wish I knew who sent me this dream: 'Tammy (or Lai-Ming?), I had a dream about you last night. You were managing a restaurant and were very busy. I couldn't understand why you would become a restaurateur in addition to all the other things you do—teaching, editing, writing, loving—but I figured it is best not to interfere. I went to the opening, you and your colleagues were working and I just tried to be quiet. But there was a big mistake with the food, the cook had not prepared the potatoes right. It did not seem like such a good restaurant. At some point you and a friend of yours (who was also one of the restaurant owners) and I went to buy candy. I hesitated to pay for the candy, because I didn't want to subsidise your failing restaurant business. But then it turned out that you wanted the candy for *yourself*, so I cordially offered to pay after all. But you had already paid. You didn't need my money (and what else could I offer?) Then your friend got shot for no reason. And we needed to catch a train, but we were late. And we got into the wrong train or bus. And then I woke up.'

'Good night, my little Brussels sprout.'

I wear the world map as though it's a dress. You can touch me on Hong Kong.

On the street where his gym is there is a bookshop called Le Merle moqueur (The Mockingbird) and a café called Le Colibri (The Hummingbird) though this odd coincidence might be lost on French speakers.

'We are fucked' is not very difficult English to master.

'I am going to bed now, my little miraculous medal.'

The horrible thought that one can walk past any number of people without knowing any of their names. The narcissism of this thought.

Making proving people wrong our goal.

Did you know? Humans are the only mammals that can't breathe and swallow at the same time. Did you know? Mosquitoes prefer biting people who are inebriated. Did you know? There are tongue prints.

'Good night my little duffel bag.'

It is not misunderstanding but partial understanding. One has to guard one's story, one's history, so much, these days.

Your games are so small I need a microscope to see them.

Some say distance makes the hearts fonder. Some say out of sight, out of mind.

On language fluency: I know it when I hear it.

I sometimes feel like I am a yew tree whose roots have been cemented.

The Chinese government hasn't censored the temperature in Hong Kong yet.

'I am going to bed now, my little doubloon.'

I should have been born with bigger breasts. I am the kind of woman who would ask people to describe me in five adjectives.

In a Chinese restaurant in Europe. I imagine all is a cover up for some illicit business. The entire family fled China. Duck tongues. Aubergine. Like a film by Jia Zhangke. Takeaway, not good. The sauces congeal quickly. The woman is like a gangster woman. You are the only foreigner when we get in. And I am the only Chinese when we leave. I order chicken feet, thinking they were going to be chilied but they were chilled. The woman who speaks exaggerated accented Italian. The husband knows nothing.

An old Cantonese pop song can be the music that ignites my memory when I am old and have dementia.

'I am off to bed now. I love you, my little artichoke heart.'

It is exhausting when you deal with walls.

My father wanted to be more handsome, perhaps. But the mole, after it
was removed, left a faint dent. Where was it? On his right cheek... if I
remember correctly. It only now exists in memory and old photos that you
cannot zoom in to. When I was small I was myself made fun of because of
the mole that sits in my philtrum. If I die, my mole will tell you it's me.

Should I give you an old pair of high heels to remember me by? Of
course not.

Slept for a bit and dreamt of naked us in a room of empty frames; we
are mid-conversation, not an argument, but somehow you are hurt and I
console you. I ask "Look at me. Do you know?" You give a non-smile, like
you sometimes do. And then I woke up. I am sleepy again now.

Will I dream once more of your eyebrows?

'I must sleep. Good night, my little pumpkin seed.'

WEBBER

4 3 2 1

Tales of Departure

i.

My sister's friend knows a friend who knows someone whose job was to
locate missing people. For a few years, she was confided to many inside
stories of moderately rich families and she retrieved teenagers and adults
alike from dire or humuliating situations. She enjoyed an odd sense of
satisfaction mingled with hatred whenever someone thanked her for
unearthing the precise location of a lost soul in the sunset of everlasting
disappointment. One day, she was gone. Nobody knew where she went.
Perhaps she wanted to be found by someone like herself; and the two of
them could be best friends, sharing strategies and evil secrets. But no one
seems to care about her enough to take the initiative to consult a detective.
And therefore she is free. Somewhere between this world and the next.

ii.

If a man claimed that she did not know her life was approaching its end,
he was lying. She knew, oh of course she knew how her inside was rotting
at a great speed. She felt by day she's wearing her inside inside-out and
by night she was really coughing her inside out. That night, wrapped in
strings of plastic water-proof batteried light bulbs, she jumped into the sea.
From afar, her body was transformed into moving fireworks igniting the
curiosity of billions of sea salts.

iii.

A very dear friend of mine (he called himself Joshua Burdette, which is
really a made-up name) liked quoting lyrics. Once, when I was telling him
about my family background, which was (and is still) not priviledged,
his bearded face twisted a little (a sign that he remembered some relevant
lyrics), and then he's reciting a song by Stevie Wonder, "Living Just
Enough for the City". Joshua spoke words that I have never spoken;
but afterwards I found that he spoke my heart; and he's much more
prolific. A lazy afternoon, we sat on a bench next to a rusted iron fence
without enjambment. We were chatting like birds of two different species,
complaining about other animals' foodlore. Suddenly he leaned forward
(and downward as well, for he's a great deal taller than me) and kissed me
on the forehead. In his unique mumbled fashion, he told me he will leave
the town and fish for a lifetime. I have never seen him since; but I hope he
fishes well, and fishes much.

Julian And James

Only when I was at home could I be away from the horror, the horror of dogs. Julian, my husband, bought an apartment which overlooked Victoria Harbour for us after we went out for three seasons: a season of courting, a season of doubting and a season of agreeing. Before, he rented a flat in Causeway Bay with a friend also from Canada. They paid HK\$30, 000 a month for it. That's not expensive for *gweilos*; they usually make good money here. But the fact was, Julian was paying most of the rent with his top salary and handsome housing allowance from the law firm.

Julian and I didn't know that the apartment building had so many dogs. But there's a park nearby with a few well-designed dog tracks. There's even a 'dog club' at the apartment for its upper-crust residents. Naturally, dog-lovers were drawn to this building. The dogs could smell my fear of them and their owners, I was sure, could observe the same. But making my fear known and visible didn't mean that the fear would miraculously evaporate or people would be sympathetic. In fact, my neighbours were having more 'dog-walking parties' than ever those days, I felt. Every time I went out or came back home I encountered unleashed dogs. Some of them were strays; they were there for the community and free food from generous housewives.

It was not possible to complain about my fear to Julian anymore. In the first few months, he would come home after work and pick me up before we went out for dinner or a movie. I was most attracted to his voice when he said 'I'll be there soon' on the phone: mid-air, conclusive, gentle. When time crawled through the humidity and heat, I stayed in the apartment and watched the daylight fade until he was home. Sometimes, I was demonstrably grateful; I would peel off his shirt and give him a massage I learnt from my aunt in Shenzhen. Then, walking to the MTR station or the taxi stand, I would clutch onto his arm. Like Moses he parted the sea of dogs for both of us to walk past.

Julian eventually grew tired of my weakness. As in tales of sore love and non-amendable relationships: there's only so much patience in even the most loving individuals. He thought I must combat my fear and learn to live with my enemies. 'Kathy, if you can't kill them, make friends with them!'

he yelled at me. I tried to be, or at least pretended to be, more at ease and more aloof, when I saw the dogs. But every time when I got close to the animals, a button inside me seemed to be automatically pressed, triggering a series of irrational responses, and reminding me of mountain dogs and tearing flesh on my little shins: a sharp pain cut into the bones when I cried all the way back to my family camping site seventeen years ago.

One Sunday, I came home after dinner with my parents in Yuen Long. When I opened the door, there was a snow white puppy with large round eyes wagging his tail at my feet. At that instant, I wanted to shut the door and leave. But Julian forced me back into the apartment. He squeezed my arm, gave me a peck on the forehead, and said he needed to get some Lucky Strikes from the 7-11 by the MTR station and that he expected to see me when he got back. Then he left me with the dog in the apartment with four walls painted sunflower yellow.

So that was his ultimate plan to help me with my fear of dogs: to shut me in with a puppy so that I could get used to its larger cousins. There I was, inside a massive enclosed box, with a dog. As if it had lost interest in me, the dog started to play with a leg of the Latin armchair; its small tail was stiff, like a little upward-pointing stick. Standing next to the window, I was stiff too. Indescribable fear banged on my stomach, waist, thighs, wrists, head, and even hair-roots. My heart hovered and twisted, skipping several beats. I prayed: as long as that small thing kept to itself within the domain of the armchair, and I within the comfort zone of the window, we'd be fine.

But the dog abandoned the armchair and walked around, on impulse, and sniffed first, the red Turkish carpet, then, my toes. I jumped and pushed it away with my foot. Then it walked back to me. Then I kicked it. I kicked it again and again and again until it was whimpering weakly; I was like a malfunctioning robot, programmed to do the nastiest thing. It happened in a split second. It was uncertain violence, visible unease. At that point, Julian came back. He had forgotten his wallet.

Julian realised what happened and yelled at me. Then this screaming monster inside me was conjured up. She took the shape of me, discarding all reason. She made inaudible sounds of accusations and unlocked the doors of those many silent tears. She thrust my body onto the concrete floor, bruising my knees and forehead. She threatened to linger on the windowsill, and eventually jump.

After that outburst, the puppy was sent away; neither of us mentioned dogs again. That became one of the taboos in our relationship.

* * *

I almost called James's name and I was ashamed. But Julian didn't know. He continued to enjoy the doggy style which always gave him maximum pleasure. Afterwards, I had a shower and when I was washing my face, I noticed some of his hairs on my facial towel. Obviously Julian had shaved before he approached me, and he was using my towel again. All of a sudden I felt a fierce disgust; I flushed the towel down the toilet and didn't regret it. When I returned to bed Julian was already asleep, snoring solidly after the bottle of wine or two he probably had during a leisurely dinner with clients.

I was mostly sleepless that night, too excited at the prospect of seeing James the next morning. We were just starting with physical explorations after a few weeks of lips-sealed text messaging. He still lived in Causeway Bay, but in a smaller apartment about five minutes' walk from Times Square. It's in an old 'Tang' building which had only five storeys. There were quite a few dazzling bird cages, mostly rustic brown, some lacking occupants, hung on the windows, presumably by older residents of the building. There were no elevators, but the back stairs were decent and there were pots of seasonal flora on every corner arranged by the landowner, who was also a gardener.

Later in our hushed relationship, James and I saw each other three days a week. I went to his place in the morning because he worked in the afternoon. Yet like a morning bird, he woke up early and brewed the best coffee for me. Sometimes Julian and James went for drinks in Lan Kwai Fong or at *Joyce is not Here* and I joined them too. On those occasions I had prickles all down my spine: I was scared that the secret in the bag would be let out and cripple my wealthy life. A burning book, a corpse and a camel were things that couldn't be hidden. There were others: I was afraid betrayal was one.

After Julian went to work in the morning, I wasted no time and left home, usually before nine. There were always a few dogs going about their business in the birdsong hours on the path which led to the main gate of the apartment building. I tip-toed my way to the taxi stand, drawing as little attention from the dogs as possible. Then I took a taxi to Times Square and from there I walked to James's place. Relaxed and content, I walked against the tide of people, too familiar with the morning hustle and bustle: men and women in business suits and students in uniforms.

The stairs to James's apartment were perfect to walk on. I enjoyed the sound my high-heels created on them (knock-knock-knock) before I was at last standing in front of his wooden door. Sometimes, I walked alone, and there would be distant music drifting over the doorjamb, or he'd be playing the piano and I'd hear that too. Other times, there was silence, and I would get worried. Then, when I opened the door, I'd see him sitting back on the sofa, reading a limited edition book, or sketching something with crayons on his notepad, and he smiled to me, his hair a bit messy, and I was relieved. Sometimes I reckoned, walking on the stairs, alone, was the very first part of our foreplay. That sexiness, that noise; somewhere between my legs began to shudder. That excitement.

There, I took off my wedding ring and there was a ring of non-tanned skin on my finger which reminded me equally of Julian and the Aesop's Fable "The Dog and the Wolf": I was the pathetic dog who preferred to be a fat slave rather than a starved vagabond.

James and I didn't do anything magnificent, only conventional lovers' activities of consuming films and being intimate. We were free like two flying birds in the direction of New Guinea. When I drew the purple curtains open, left and right, below vehicles were swooping. There was no clustering or barking of dogs, only laughing teenagers and 'ding-ding' from slowly-passing trams to Central. It surprised me every time when I laid flat on my back, and James shivered inside me, helpless, kissing my neck. On the third floor, that tiny apartment felt like heaven. Or an infinite space for togetherness.

At home, when I was away from home.

Ann

Everybody smiled. Everybody moved a step forward. Everybody smiled again. How splendid the weather was. How happy little Annie was. She remembers her red dress, John's blue canvas shoes with a team of ants climbing up and down (orange juice!), May's smart yellow socks, Mama's touch on her head. But then the touch was not decorated by delightful colours. It was plain. John and May smiled at their Papa, Uncle Brian. Uncle Brian was taking photos of them...one, another one, and then another one... with appreciation. Little Annie did not understand why she was not allowed to stand between John and May. Red matches blue and yellow bloody well; but she wasn't included in any of the pictures.

Miss Wong gave Ann a slice of cake. Ann remembers her orange dress: it was too short to cover the knees and she kept pulling and pulling (The bruises!).

Nicolas and Peter laughed at her. Soon Margaret, Paul, Liz, Lydia and Susan joined the activity free of charge. She pulled even harder. The bruises embarrassed her less than the act of hiding them, Ann thinks. But Ann was still small and she did not know. She retreated to the washroom and cursed her Mama for picking such a wretched dress (Don't I have another orange dress!), sincerely forgetting that Mama did not know she fell from the bicycle and bruised her knees. Since she was given the permission to wash her own body, no one but Ann knows that she is quite unfit for looking after herself. Miss Wong gave Ann a slice of birthday cake when she returned to the hall. The birthday song (Shall we all live, we shall live all, all live shall we, live all we shall) was sung already. Photos were already taken. Ann wondered how they could forget her. She was one of the birthday fairies: she was Orange Cutie. How could the other six students make out of themselves? Without her, a rainbow's not a rainbow.

Carol liked shrimp flavour potato chips and Jenny... Jenny liked milk chocolate bars. They told jokes and some of them did amuse Ann--the boys were funny, even Jack the bookworm knew how to make Ann laugh and employed himself sometimes in winking his right single-eyelidded eye (Left eye didn't work!). Ann did not usually have such a good time. Workload was rather heavy and she was reluctantly interested in busying herself in studies though she understood that concentrating too much on textbooks strengthened her short-sightedness. Tom, Patrick, Carol, Ben, Jack and Jenny gathered at Ann's house to work on a term project thanks to Mr. Cheung's arrangement. They were half way through and the boys suggested fetching some snacks from the supermarket. Ann remembers she opened the door for the guys and pointed to them the way to the shopping mall, all of the time she was thinking how wonderful she looked in the new yellow dress and how the boys must notice that if they were not blind. Before leaving, the boys asked Ann what she thought Carol and Jenny would want to have. Ann replied with a fierce expectation and was about to tell them she wanted marshmallow with fruit juice inside, only to find that they had no grateful intention to know her preferences. They left, and at that point denied the fragile confidence Ann had imagined she had. The boys were not blind but no doubts she was not in their minds. Ann reproached, how yellow makes your hollow cheeks hollower!

How sad! Jim was the teacher. A not so convincing one (He's short!) but he knew how to play and that's okay. On Ann's twentieth birthday Mama bought her a guitar green of colour. From Venice! From London! From Paris! No no... from Beijing! Brand new Rock and Roll production designed by singer Faye Wong's ex-boyfriend's musical partner's ex-wife Siu Yu Yan. What a lovely lovely guitar, Ann thought. Ann remembers she asked Jim to teach her how to play the guitar. She was a little bit too shy to learn in a class: students with varied talents would stress her very much. Jim answered playfully: 'Perhaps, perhaps, perhaps', easily disappointing Ann to death. Everyday she thought of one reason why Jim refused to earn some extra pocket money and when the reasons collected more or less reached the number 100 Jim called. She put down the phone and wept. Oh after all she's not that hateful, her hands were not too small, she was not tremendously ugly, her hair did not look like a wig, it's right to trim her fingernails every now and then, her buttocks weren't too small like a little boy's, her voice did not sound like a ten-year old girl asking for marshmallow, she was not too dull, her nose did not have too many black dots, she did not wear dresses tastelessly, she did not smile with too many teeth shown, she... Ann was relieved, her self-esteem rose to its highest level in years. The first lesson took place in Ann's bedroom and Sarah also came. Sarah did not have her own guitar but she was always holding a green one. Ann turned green and was absolutely green when she saw Sarah stroked the neck of the guitar and struck the strings with her slender fingers. Jim wanted to teach Sarah, not Ann. Ann once again played the 'Best Supporting Role'. Not so new to the job.

Ann's friend Jane already had two babies. Rose was then pregnant. Elina was married, divorced, married again (Same man!). Helen emigrated to Ireland with her husband, Adam. But they were back long time ago. Alice still dreamt day and night and Amanda was getting married with Vicent. Ann remembers she wore a long blue dress on their wedding ceremony. The couple wanted something 'different' and the maid of honour, Yvette, thought of a 'blue' wedding. The guests all wore blue, light or dark. How strange it felt, to see everybody so dumbly obeyed the artificial rule, yet seemed so at home about it. Ann was glad to see her friends again, though no one appeared to recognize her, or to come and talk to her and ask her how's she doing. In the church she sat on the last pew, in the party she felt blue by leaning against the wall staring at the fake big wedding cake offered by the hotel, when George, Joe, Veronica, Lilian, Zoey, Kimmy, Ray, Felix, Snoopy, Kitty, Simpson... danced she looked.

Smiled. Moved a step forward. Smiled again. Mona then ran about the fountain, how red suited her. Mona picked up a snail and kissed its shell (Hey Mona!). Sam only looked on and laughed. What a lovely daughter and a boyish husband. How splendid the weather was. How happy Ann was. In a sharp purple dress Ann was so pretty, oh but Mona and Sam ran into the labyrinth without asking her to join...

The Sisters' Bed

When she was small she shared a bed with her younger sister. It was not really a bed but a large sofa in the living room. Now the sisters were approaching the age of autumn; the sofa was still kept by the family. The young people called it the 'picnic sofa' and feasted on it.

While You Are Away

I wait for your calls which come at unexpected hours. Other times, I may drink wine. I admit it: I chose the cheapest bottle in the supermarket today. I didn't know what to pick. The vegetarian beers you left in the fridge were pathetic. I guess I must have grown three years since you left; the cashier didn't ask my age.

How can I eat all the pears you bought me? Now they are so soft, best for toothless grannies. I shall not touch the bananas. They don't look healthy, at all. And stacked microwaved meals in the freezer are like cold cases. You taught me how to make coffee, but the coffee I make is either too bitter or like water.

I hang your blue shirts everywhere in the flat. Yes, even the checked 'tablecloth' shirt. I hide those I don't like. It's a lie that clothes smell of people. I can't smell you when I press the sleeves upon my nose. Environmentally-friendly washing powder is all.

Now that no one competes with me for the use of the bathroom sink, I no longer want to brush my teeth elaborately. I only do those many steps to annoy you.

I would pay to smell your after-meal burps. I would pay to hear your ten o'clock snores.

Fisherwoman In A Storm

I have been trapped in this boat for nights. How many? The eternal moon, much praised by poets and romantics, may know but I have lost count.

Old husbands' tale: when you smell brewed oolong, steamed shrimps or egg yolk in a mooncake, in a shrilling storm, in the open sea, you are hallucinating. Cow-head and horse-face are going to get you.

But apart from the sea and more sea, I smell nothing else. Salt is my every drop of saliva, my sweat, my skin. The fish I had caught are now dead; their corpses, dishevelled, shine dully together. Their eyes are careless: they have no agony.

I do see myself walking home with the day's dead catch. The door to our brick house is only several steps away—I can almost touch it! How white the walls are, on the outside. My father painted them for the previous Lunar New Year. But I cannot see the inside. It is dark like a swallowed night except for a pale speck. My mother is still warming the stove, cooking rice, waiting for me.

I want to go home.

Grandma

My grandma was toothless for as long as I could remember. She carried a pair of sharp scissors whenever she went to a restaurant to mince food into suitably tiny pieces: steamed chicken breast, fried broccoli, curry squid, etc. One afternoon, when she was preparing dinner in the kitchen, grandma accidentally chopped off her right index finger. How that happened was now unimaginable. She managed to call an ambulance quickly; but the finger could no longer be redeemed. After the event, grandma was physically weak. She refused to cook again and claimed that her world was now monochromatic. Her six children, my mom included, came to a consensus to send her to a home for the elderly. They said that was only a temporary measure. Like many other temporary decisions, the arrangement became permanent.

The home for the elderly was near where I worked and lived. Therefore, I was able to visit grandma everyday. Even in the first week, grandma's hair was more unkempt than before. She also gave up dying her hair and putting different kinds of lotion on her face. Within a month she had a full head of wild pearly strands like a mermaid who asked for immortality with eagerness but unwittingly forgot to demand perpetual youth. She was still beautiful, I thought, for an eighty-year-old woman, even though she seemed to have grown weary of her looks and was no longer proud of her tailor-made flower-pattered cheongsams.

I was twenty-two years old that year, and worked full-time in a day-care centre looking after young kids when their lower-middle-class parents went to battle in brightly-lit and dully-decorated offices. It was a huge consolation to just sit there with grandma in almost absolute quietness after prolonged exposure to shrieks and screams and loud giggles. Grandma's room was neat, carpeted and had mullioned glass windows that generously absorbed the scene of a small street outside. Every now and then there was a pleasant whiff of fresh bread and chocolate cookies. Her six children were not thrifty about their mother's final earthly lodging.

Grandma started talking about her lost finger the following year. It was one gloomy Saturday, a typhoon irresponsibly left behind a cracked grey sky featuring kaleidoscopic lightning and a massive amount of rain that smelt strangely of animal blood. I peeled an orange for grandma after she had finished an early dinner of cut spring rolls and lukewarm pork congee. She extended her right hand, ambidextrous as she was, and tried to fetch that slice of juicy orange with her thumb and index finger, obviously forgetting that the latter was no more than a sprout of human flesh, its development brutally arrested by her own momentous wrongdoing. The slice dropped onto the floor before I could catch it.

Grandma lost appetite for the orange and asked for Oolong tea instead. As if I was the culprit of the mild fiasco, I felt inexplicably guilty and became speechless. Perhaps I was also a little bit angry. Why was she so incompetent? I really thought after one year grandma should have already grown accustomed to the finger's absence.

An embarrassing fifteen minutes passed, she sitting upright and I standing next to her like an intimidated maid in her probation period. Then grandma asked if I thought losing a finger was similar to losing a child. Baffled, I expressed ignorance by knitting my eyebrows and producing lots of wrinkles on my forehead. Grandma pointed at the empty space between her thumb and middle finger and swore there existed a ghost finger, haunting her, just like her ghost first child. She must have lost her mind, I thought. Her first child was my mother! She gave birth to her in the toilet of the village hospital in Hubei when she was twenty-one. That was the most well-known joke in the family. My mom's younger sisters and brothers each had more elegant ways to make their first appearance in this clumsy world.

Grandma said enormous years kept sliding out of her grip, and that she was referring to the first child, the aborted one, not my mother. She got pregnant in the same year when she started having her menstruation. The bleeding crotch was warm and dripped patterns on her underwear. The father of the unborn baby was her then best friend's farmer brother, all sweaty and stiff muscles. I felt extremely uncomfortable with this piece of information she had just irrevocably fed me. Why me? Why was I chosen to bear her secrets? Because I was her eldest grandchild? Once started, grandma would not stop recounting her past. Like the rain outside, her tale was persistent and passionate, forming small streams of freckled mirrors and roadside dust.

She was only fourteen years old. Her hair was tied up in her favourite
gingerly pony tail, and her legs smooth with unshaved fine hairs. She
enlisted the best friend to help with the abortion while the baby's father
was 'kept inside a drum', as the Chinese idiom graphically goes. The
scene was not very bloody, grandma boasted, and continued to talk
about long ropes and blunt knives. I told her I was not interested in the
details, too disgusted about the whole affair. Grandma and her best friend,
due to shame or maturity, could not speak to each other anymore after
the 'surgery'. That friendship was gone; so vulnerable was the teenage
bond. Grandma compared the boyfriend and herself to two trains going
in opposite directions on parallel tracks but meeting instantaneously to
produce electric sparks in their vicinity.

The lost finger reminded grandma of that ghost child, now resurfaced after
being absent for almost half a century. The unborn baby had also conjured
up the involuntary memory of other children she had selfishly abandoned
before coming to Hong Kong, she said. Without them, her life was now
incomplete. They were like holes in a supposedly perfect quilt. I was
shocked: what 'other' children? 'Children'? Was there more than one?

Grandma embarked the fishing boat for Sha Tau Kok with a cast of
villagers who were in their twenties and thirties. The year was 1957—
everyone was starving and shooting hostile gazes at those who were
fortunate enough to have food and did not resemble skeletons. The night
before, she had sent her two daughters to a distant aunt's house on a
hillside; the house was partly made of straw and cow dung, looking west.
Grandma never considered retrieving the girls, even though the whole
time when she was on the cramped boat saturated with an agglomeration
of hope and loss she was thinking of their long eyelashes like their dead
father's. She held her cloth bag tightly on her lap—inside, the remains of
some summer clothes and a few pieces of broken jewellery her mother had
endowed to her.

The suppressed past was ripped up, grandma said. About five years ago,
the two daughters who were still living in Hubei sent her a handwritten
letter, asking for some money so that they could travel to Hong Kong and
reunite with their biological mother. The letter weighed so lightly and yet
so heavily in grandma's palm. Out of horror, fear and self-condemnation,
she wrote back to tell them there was no need to meet, since her entire
happy family was now in Hong Kong. Perhaps she wanted only to

be known by this invented and partial identity—a mother of six and grandmother of seven. She had no strength to cling to the past; instead, she was to purge it. Grandma also cruelly asked the two daughters not to contact her again or beg for money. She said she burnt the letter; snuffed fire was the sad heart.

I was utterly confused. One of these daughters must be my mother. According to the family legend that was often repeated at festival gatherings, my mom was born in a village hospital, the year before grandma was illegally tossing and turning—swimming like a butterfly—in the formidable Hong Kong waters.

Grandma said she gave birth to a stillborn, the first child of the nameless man with unforgettable eyelashes, in the toilet of their house. In a toilet, but not in a hospital toilet. A baby, but not my mother. The anecdote was misunderstood and misattributed to my mom after several retellings.

Does she know? I asked. Grandma beckoned me to refill her cup with some more Oolong tea. The sky was completely dark outside, more apparitions were hauling up. She said not only did my mom know that she was not born in a toilet; she also knew that she was only a half-sister to her siblings. The three of them: my mother, her father (it should be 'step-father'—my beloved grandfather who died when I was fifteen), and grandma had kept this secret for their whole life, as, if her brothers and sisters knew about the truth they would not respect my mom as much. I always wondered why my mom did not have the Chinese character, Lai, in her name. My aunts were called Lai-Fan, Lai-San and Lai-Lan; my uncles were called Lai-Man and Lai-Dan. The word 'Lai' is a noun, it means 'encouragement'. My mom's name was 'Yan-Hong', a red swallow, a swallow soaked in blood.

That perhaps was a more appropriate name for grandma. Like a swallow she flew from one place to another either for escape or for livelihood. And she had blood on her hands in her teenage days when she ultimately rejected a baby's entrance to life. In her old age, she regretfully dismissed and humiliated her own blood.

A handful of children: some male, some female; some tall, some short; some older, some younger; some dead, some living; some in Hubei, some had planted themselves in Hong Kong; some probably loved grandma, some didn't. Ten of them in total, all of them were once in her womb with great expectations. Now, except those who died prematurely, everyone had a different destiny, adding new branches and new secrets to the same family tree forked like meandering rivers.

Grandma died the month before she turned eighty-five. Her openly-acknowledged children and grandchildren were all by her bed when she lay dying. I imagined in her last waking moments she touched the ghost finger and apologized.

A week later, grandma was buried with her right index finger which had been preserved in the hospital.

Random Fragments From All These Years

One day I wrote her name upon the strand,
But came the waves and washed it away[.]
—Edmund Spenser

i.

Union of the upper and lower lips:
you like *bamboo, member, paper,*
and many more: random words
you whisper in my ears from multiple
rudimentary and spontaneous scripts.
The unveiled night seems perpetual
and perpetually ours. Meanings are
arbitrary, unnecessary. Perhaps—perhaps,
in both time yet to come and time afore,
this sensual game of earlobe-warming
with words—words that precede
and succeed us—was played, is played,
will be played in the eternal present.

ii.

Summer smeared my face with melting butter. Thirteen dinners after the
first Indian meal, tonight was a delightful compound of white wine, over-
cooked chicken breasts and cheesecakes. I told myself I must remember this:
being held by you, finally, on your bed: kissed, touched, licked, squeezed
and fucked. All verbs sublimely passive and telling of passionate physical
gifts. When you fly away—for you are a frequent flyer and majestic liar—
what I remember is useful: fingers, index and middle, tiptoe swiftly on
somewhere wrinkled until an impatiently self-inflicted orgasm. How I want
you to know this; how I want you to echo this brilliance of sorrow.

iii.

This morning were you warming your feet? How? Who else was involved?
For how long? Do you play with the snow which is never seen in Hong

Kong? A snowman with a pointy nose in a fairytale in a glass ball. Absence of years. I mean ears. Why aren't you writing? Because I say silly things? Because I say things I mean? Do you light cinnamon-scented candles on your dinner table? Do you hold someone when watching Wong Ka Wai's *2046*? Do you still wear a white T-shirt whenever you feel sinister? Is that a protest against terrorism, war, and sending a Chinese into Space? Do you look out of the window and pray that someone would delightfully appear, a flash of an image, and plant you a kiss on the lips? Which is more in this world? Love, or raindrops? Which is longer? Our distance, or this particular evening when you are absent? Two time zones—clocks' arms understand and pickpocket us—yet my now is your present.

iv.

The stairs to your apartment are perfect to walk on. I enjoy the clear sound my high-heels create on them—knock-knock-knock—before I am at last standing in front of your wooden door. Most of the times, I walk alone, and there is distant music drifting over the doorjamb, or you are playing the piano and I hear that too. Other times, there is silence, and I get worried. Then, when I open the door, I see you sitting back on the sofa, reading a limited edition book, or sketching something with crayons on your notepad, and you smile to me, your hair is a bit messy, and I am relieved. Sometimes I reckon, walking on the stairs, alone, is the very first part of our foreplay. That sexiness, that boasting noise, somewhere between my thighs begins to shudder. That untamed excitement.

v.

You have noticed, in this poem 'you' always refers to you. You have no name. Names are burdensome, names identify. You'll remain anonymous, mysterious. I pray that some day in the future, your shadow, slender and speechless, will collide with mine again. Long live logophilia; sexphilia; youphilia. It is not forgiveness I ask for, but un-forgetfulness. One afternoon before Death stops his chariot for me, I will make a bonfire and burn all those heyday e-mail correspondences I have printed and stored in a locked closet. Dickens did not want to preserve words from Collins, Tennyson and Thackeray, why should I keep you and me for posterity? Burning; let us choose fire over ice. Not stupidities that are destroyed, nor fears; but unpleasant surprises for our separate offspring of different hues of darkness. Who's deciding how much of us should survive?

vi.

One sleepless night
I dreamt of you. And hey there
was also your bob-haired wife,
a silhouetted shape from my
imagination: the two of you sleep
on the same bed, dream two different
little dreams. That's acting,
and thus that's art. How peculiar—
I didn't cry or feel uneasy. Not at all
absorbed by this repetitively
dislocated imagery.

vii.

Tell me things, such as: if you ever get a tattoo, would it say 'I love Bella'?
The words stained under a picture of a non-demolished Star Ferry Pier or
a woman with breasts like ice-cream cubes. Tell me things, including why
in anger you switch off the phone and why you want a girlfriend who
can write but not dance, or sing. Is performing with words better and less
intimidating? Tell me things, for example: how you know I love strawberry
milkshakes and burnt chicken wings instead of Claret and T-bone steaks.
Tell me things. Tell me things. Tell me. Tell me. Tell. Tell. Tell.

viii.

The same day I sat facing you in the kitchen with greasy Indian food
displayed in front of us, Prince Charles and Chris Patten sailed out of
Victoria Harbour in the Royal Yacht Britannia. It was the first time I dined
with you after numerous false starts and coy emails written with decorum.
Half past eight in the evening, eyes were still adjusting the wondrous
closeness of the other's dilated pupils. I listened attentively to your words
and in a moment of drowsiness, the consonants and heavy vowels seemed
to sit on the four corners of the table, lingering, mocking my ineloquence.
Towards the end of our glistening meal, you said to me, 'You are the only
one' and I was afraid. I was afraid that you were drunk.

ix.

You do not like to have hair, ice cream and semen on the floor or on the sofa or on the mattress. You are angry when you discover them and poor black strong hair poor sweet ice cream poor milky semen are picked up or wiped away in haste. Then you look at me, you are still slightly angry, and I can't help laughing. You fall in love with a younger girl and you know you have to tolerate some things. Not just hair and ice cream and semen carelessly found on the floor, but also slammed doors, giggles, Cantonese colloquial 'your head' and unreasonable complaints: I cannot guarantee I will be a better person when I grow older, but love me anyway, love me.

x.

A novelist can spend a whole chapter on whether the main character— male—wants to buy nail-polish and after fifty pages he decides not to buy it, so why can't I use the last section of this story to tell you why I like having your tongue dance with mine? Now look, your tongue is rather ordinary, but I like it anyway because it makes me realize that in more than fifty years' time, when I am in a crowded elevator and everyone's face is younger and more innocent than mine, I can still stand straight and smile to myself thinking of the taste and roughness of your tongue. Nothing is going to steal this memory from me. Not time. Not *1984*-ish government policies. Not age. Not even your death which will come sooner or later. No.

Tammy Ho Lai-Ming is a founding co-editor of *Cha: An Asian Literary Journal* and the academic journal *Hong Kong Studies* (Chinese University Press), English Editor of *Voice & Verse Poetry Magazine*, and the Vice President of PEN Hong Kong. She has co-edited several poetry anthologies, including *Desde Hong Kong: Poets in Conversation with Octavio Paz* (2014), *Quixotica: Poems East of La Mancha* (2016), *Twin Cities: An Anthology of Twin Cinema from Singapore and Hong Kong* (2017), and her literary translations have been published in *World Literature Today*, *Chinese Literature Today*, *Pathlight*, *Drunken Boat*, and by the Chinese University Press. Her first poetry collection is *Hula Hooping* (Chameleon Press, 2015). She is currently an Associate Professor at Hong Kong Baptist University and she has single-authored academic books forthcoming from Palgrave and Springer. She is a recipient of the Hong Kong Arts Development Council's Young Artist Award in Literary Arts.